W9-BSD-490

For Dad
and
"an india-rubber ball"

Thanks to everyone at Viking who helped make this book possible.

VIKING
Published by the Penguin Group
Penguin Books USA Inc., 375 Hudson Street, New York, New York 10014, U.S.A.
Penguin Books Ltd, 27 Wrights Lane, London W8 5TZ, England
Penguin Books Australia Ltd, Ringwood, Victoria, Australia
Penguin Books Canada Ltd, 10 Alcorn Avenue, Toronto, Ontario, Canada M4V 3B2
Penguin Books (N.Z.) Ltd, 182-190 Wairau Road, Auckland 10, New Zealand

Penguin Books Ltd, Registered Offices: Harmondsworth, Middlesex, England

First published in 1994 by Viking, a division of Penguin Books USA Inc.

1 3 5 7 9 10 8 6 4 2

LIBRARY OF CONGRESS CATALOGING-IN-PUBLICATION DATA
McGuire, Richard.   Night becomes day / Richard McGuire.   p. cm.
Summary: The progress of time is illustrated by a sequence of objects
and themes, including stream/river/ocean and street/highway/bridge.
ISBN 0-670-85547-2
[1. Time—Fiction. 2. Day—Fiction.]   I. Title.
PZ7.M4786215Ni 1994 [E]—dc20   94-9923 CIP AC

Printed in Singapore
Set in Futura Medium

NIGHT
BECOMES
DAY

BY

RICHARD McGUIRE

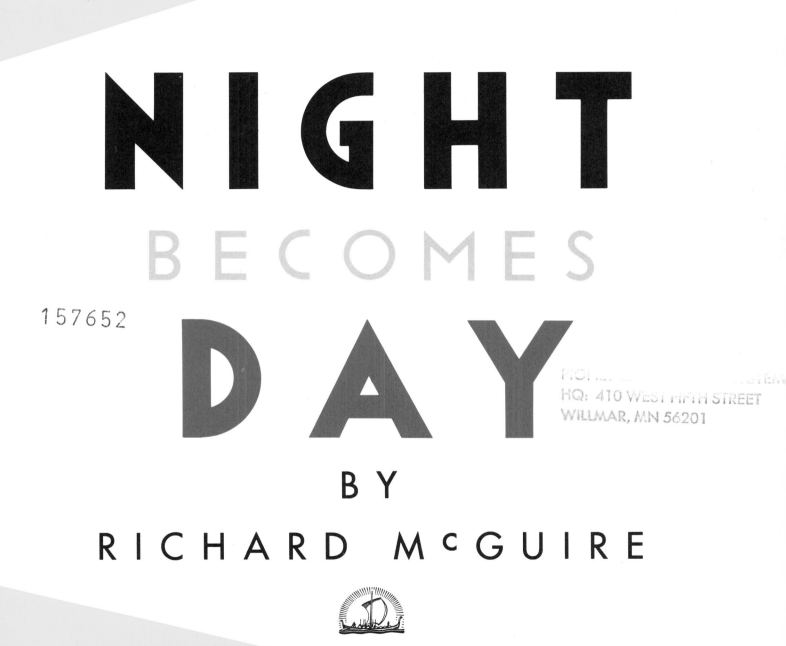

VIKING

Night becomes day

And day becomes bright

Bright becomes sun

And sun becomes shine

Shine becomes sparkle

And sparkle becomes stream

Stream becomes river

And river becomes ocean

Ocean becomes wave

And wave becomes beach

Beach becomes hill

And hill becomes mountain

Mountain becomes peak

And peak becomes valley

Valley becomes town

And town becomes street

Street becomes highway

And highway becomes bridge

Bridge becomes tunnel

And tunnel becomes city

City becomes building

And building becomes cloud

Cloud becomes rain

And rain becomes tree

Tree becomes paper

And paper becomes news

News becomes trash

And trash becomes new

New becomes birthday

And birthday becomes candle

Candle becomes smoke

And smoke becomes wind

Wind becomes cold

And cold becomes snow

Snow becomes puddle

And puddle becomes grass

Grass becomes food

And food becomes wool

Wool becomes blanket

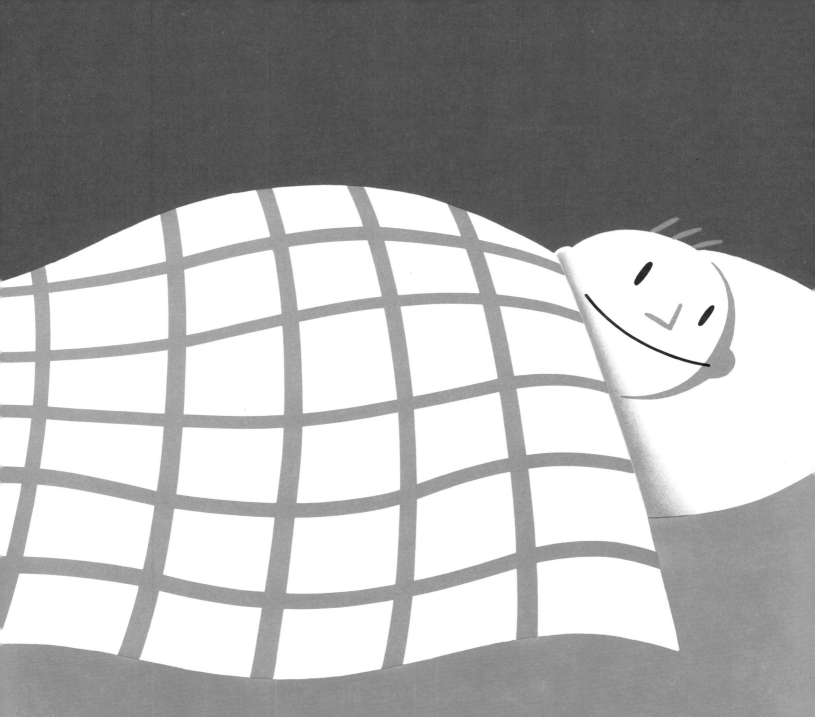

And blanket becomes warm

Warm becomes sleep

And sleep becomes dream

Dream becomes good

And good becomes night